This book belongs to:

....

....

....

....

Retold by Gaby Goldsack
Illustrated by Emma Lake

Language consultant: Betty Root

This edition published by Parragon in 2013
Parragon
Chartist House
15–17 Trim Street
Bath BA1 1HA, UK
www.parragon.com

ISBN 978-1-4454-7070-2

Printed in China

Rapunzel

Parragon

Bath • New York • Singapore • Hong Kong • Cologne • Delhi
Melbourne • Amsterdam • Johannesburg • Shenzhen

Helping your Child to Read

Learning to read is an exciting challenge for most children. From a very early age, sharing story books with children, talking about the pictures and guessing what might happen next are all very important parts of the reading experience.

Sharing reading

Set aside a regular quiet time to share reading with younger children, or to be on hand to encourage older children as they develop into independent readers.

This book is intended to encourage and support the early stages of learning to read. It is a well-loved tale that children will happily listen to again and again. Familiarity helps children to identify some of the words and phrases.

When you feel your child is ready to move on a little, encourage him or her to join in so that you read the story aloud together. Always pause to talk about the pictures. The easy-to-read speech bubbles in this book provide an excellent 'joining-in' activity. The bright, clear illustrations and matching text will help children to understand the story.

Building confidence
In time, children will want to read *to* you. When this happens, be patient and give continual praise. They may not read all the words correctly, but children's substitutions are often very good guesses.

The repetition in each book is particularly helpful for building confidence. If your child cannot read a particular word, go back to the beginning of the sentence and read it together so the meaning is not lost. Most importantly, do not continue if your child is tired or simply in need of a change.

Reading aloud
The next step is to ask your child to read alone. Try to be on hand to give help and support. Remember to give lots of encouragement and praise. This will ensure that children will find reading an enjoyable and rewarding experience.

Once upon a time, a man picked
a lettuce.

He picked it for his wife.

She was having a baby.

But the lettuce grew in the witch's garden.

The witch was cross.

"When your baby is born give it to me,

or I will punish you!" she said.

The man was scared.

He agreed to give the baby to the witch.

The man and his wife had a baby girl.

The witch took her away.

She called the baby girl Rapunzel.

Rapunzel grew up with the witch.

Her hair grew very long.

The witch hid Rapunzel in a tower.
The tower had no door or stairs.
Each day, the witch came
to the tower. She said,
    "Rapunzel, Rapunzel!
    Let down your hair."

Rapunzel let down her
long hair.
The witch climbed up
into the tower.

One day, a Prince rode by.

He heard Rapunzel singing in the tower.

"Who is singing in the tower?" he thought. "I would like to see her."

But he could not find a door.

Just then, the witch came by.

The Prince hid.

Who is singing?

The witch came to the tower.

She said,

"Rapunzel, Rapunzel!

Let down your hair."

Rapunzel let down her long hair.

The Prince watched the witch climb up.

When the witch went away, the Prince
went to the tower and said,

"Rapunzel, Rapunzel!
Let down your hair."

Rapunzel let down her long hair.
The Prince climbed up.

At first, Rapunzel was scared.
But the Prince was very kind.

The Prince and Rapunzel fell in love.

"Let's run away," said the Prince.

"But how?" asked Rapunzel.

Then she had an idea.

"Each day you come, bring some silk.
I will use the silk to make a ladder. Then
I can climb down."

Each day, the Prince came to the tower.
The witch did not know about the Prince.

Until, one day, Rapunzel forgot and said, "Witch, you hurt me. The Prince doesn't hurt me when he climbs up."

The witch was very cross.

She cut off Rapunzel's long hair.

"I will punish you!" said the witch.

And she sent Rapunzel away.

The next day, the Prince came to the
tower. He said,

      "Rapunzel, Rapunzel!
      Let down your hair."

The witch let down Rapunzel's long hair.
The Prince climbed up.
"Where is Rapunzel?" cried the Prince.
"I will punish you!" said the witch.

The witch pushed the Prince out
of the window.

He fell from the tower.

He fell on a thorny bush
and hurt his eyes.

He was blind.

The blind Prince was very sad.

He went far away.

One day, he heard singing.

He knew it was Rapunzel.

Rapunzel saw the Prince.

She began to cry with joy.

Her tears fell on the Prince's eyes.

He could see again.

Rapunzel and the Prince went back to the Prince's kingdom.

They got married and lived happily ever after.

Read and Say

How many of these words can you say? The pictures will help you. Look back in your book and see if you can find the words in the story.

garden

witch

wife

lettuce

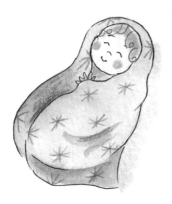

baby

Rapunzel

tower

Prince

hair

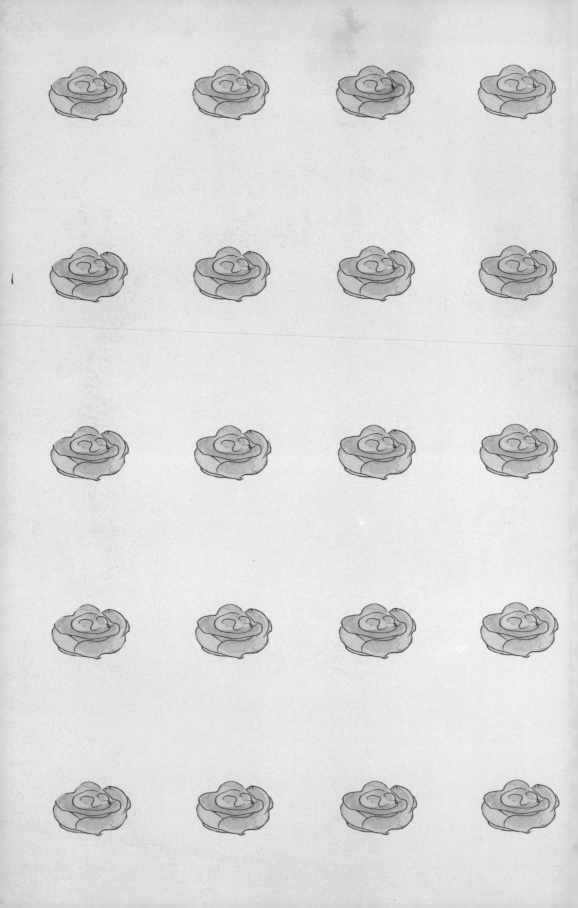